This book is dedicated to my parents, Samuel and Anne Marie Gervase, who have formed and shaped my life to become extraordinary, and taught me so many life lessons. I am grateful for their love, guidance, and inspiration through the years. It is with their encouragement that I was driven to finally write these books that I have dreamed of creating since I was 5 years old. I love you both infinitely. I am beyond blessed. This one's for you…

www.mascotbooks.com

Bella's Adventures: Turn That Frown Upside Down

©2014 Jennifer Gervase Benson. All Rights Reserved. No part of this publication may be reproduced, stored in a retrieval system or transmitted in any form by any means electronic, mechanical, or photocopying, recording or otherwise without the permission of the author.

For more information, please contact:
Mascot Books
560 Herndon Parkway #120
Herndon, VA 20170
info@mascotbooks.com

CPSIA Code: PRT1114A
ISBN-13: 978-1-62086-819-5
Library of Congress Control Number: 2014918600

Printed in the United States

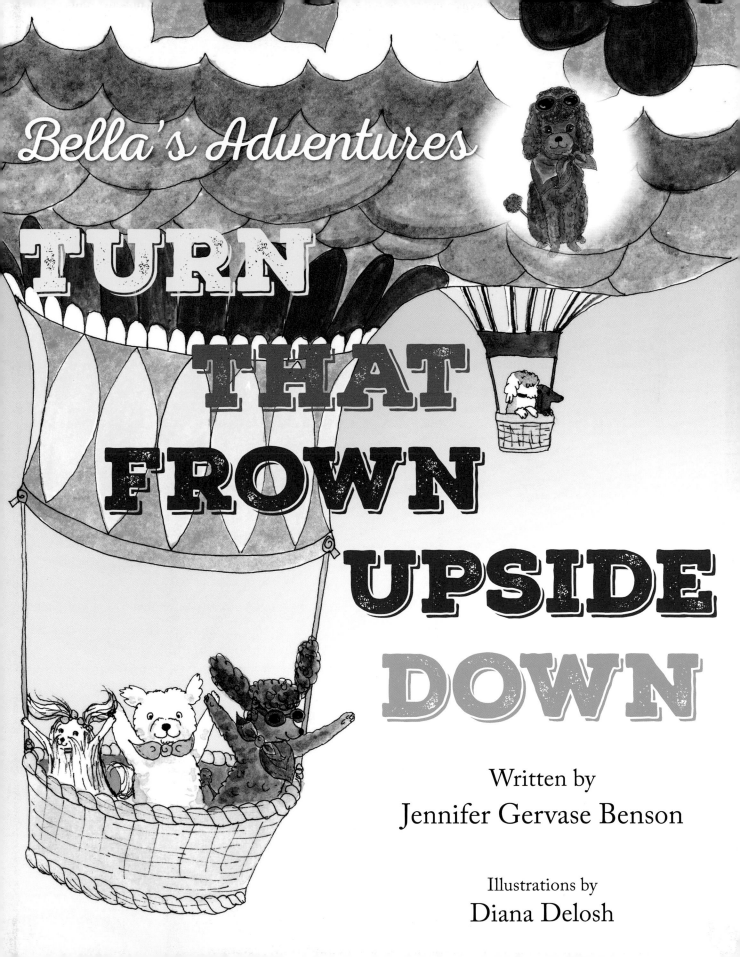

Bella's Adventures

TURN THAT FROWN UPSIDE DOWN

Written by
Jennifer Gervase Benson

Illustrations by
Diana Delosh

Bella was the smartest dog in all of Puppyville, New Bark State.
She was a red poodle that lived in a purple house with a polka-dotted gate.

The house was located on the corner of Bone Lane.
Many dogs lived there, even a Sheep Dog and Great Dane.

Bella was admired by all the other dogs in the neighborhood.
She was smart, knew all the answers, and always did what she should.

She was a cool dog, too; everyone wanted to be her friend.
Bella loved adventures, exploring, and anything fun; but always
learned good lessons in the end.

Bella's best friends were Max, the white dog up the street.
And there was Cuddles, the quiet little Maltese.

There also was Princess, the beautiful Pomeranian,
And Mario, the Chihuahua who was from the Mediterranean.

Something was always going on in Puppyville.
Those silly dogs were always seeking a thrill.

The dogs were taking a hot air balloon ride.
But not Max…today, he was feeling on the sad side.

He didn't want to participate.
He wasn't feeling so great.

Max was down on himself, not feeling positive.
He was quiet, reserved, and not very talkative.

This wasn't like Max. Usually, he was the first to go outside to play.
But today, he was just feeling glum and gray.

Bella asked Max, "What's wrong, old pal?"
Max said, "I am not sure. I think today, I have bad morale."

Soft-spoken Cuddles whispered, "What the heck is morale anyways?"
Bella said, "It's the feeling that drives good or bad days."

Bella exclaimed, "Max, turn that frown upside down!
How can we all help you to turn it around?"

Max frowned and replied, "I don't know. I'm really mad.
Today, I don't feel like a happy dog. I just feel sad.

I am not as good as the other dogs.
I'm a slow runner, and never catch the frogs.

My bark isn't the loudest.
My jumps aren't the farthest.

I don't always get the ball when we play catch.
And I always miss the bone when we play fetch."

Bella scowled, "Max, you're a GREAT friend.
You have to believe that until the end!

There are so many good things about you.
Everyone loves you through and through!"

Max said, "Bella, you HAVE to say that. You're my best friend."
Cuddles whispered, "You ARE fantastic. That's not pretend."

Max said, "Oh, I don't know.
Today, I just don't feel that is so."

Bella said, "Sometimes we wake up happy and bright.
Those days seem easy, because everything is right.

The things we say to ourselves are happy, joyful, and sunny.
Because of the positivity in our minds, we are cheerful and funny.

When we don't feel good about ourselves, it affects what we do.
What we say inside our minds is sad, unhappy, and blue.

Positive thoughts, feelings, and actions lead to more of the same kind.
It is like taking a great song and constantly hitting play and rewind!"

"Feeling bad affects our actions.
Maybe, we won't do things we like.
For instance - playing catch, swimming, hot air balloon
rides, or riding a bike.

We might get in trouble at school or get yelled at in our home.
We might fight with other dogs or be mean to the gnome.

When our thoughts and our feelings are good,
then our actions are good.
When thoughts and feelings are sad,
then the things we do are not as they should."

"How do I fix this?" Max inquisitively asked.
"Choose to be positive!" Bella tasked.

"Flip the bad to a good, squash the gloomy, and make it upbeat!
Your thoughts, feelings, and actions will soon become SWEET!

Catch yourself when you think or say a negative thing.
Reword it to be positive and happiness it will bring!"

Max decided he needed to reword all of
the previous negative thoughts he had.
He'd get rid of any thoughts that were bad.

"I'm a great dog. My game of fetch is good enough.
My bark is the best. RUFF, RUFF, RUFF!

I do try hard. I am a good frog-catcher! I love to play and run.
WOW!" he barked. "Positive self-talk really is fun!"

Max grabbed Bella's and Cuddles' paws. "It's not too late.
Let's get to the balloon launch. This is going to be great!"

They got there as fast as they could,
all three dogs running paw-in-paw.
They jumped into the balloon. As it rose,
they looked at the skyline in awe.

Looking through the sky, what a
beautiful site it was to see:
Dozens of balloons, a hundred dogs,
and Max now smiling with glee.

Max loudly barked,
"I can't believe I almost missed this adventure!"
Cuddles, Bella, and Max gave the ride two paws
up with a happy, "RAWR!"

The moral of the story is a positive self-talk lesson for us all to follow.
We need to listen to the thoughts in our minds: Are they high or low?
Are they blissful thoughts? Or in sadness, do we wallow?

Sometimes, it's a choice to be happy and bright,
Because not everything always goes right.

Make the best of the situation and choose a brighter way.
Positive thoughts need to be our choice each and every day!

We must believe: I
am good! I am great!
I can do anything!
And watch how
much happiness your
positive thoughts
will bring!

Jennifer Gervase Benson resides in Rochester, New York with her husband, Christopher. They are the proud owners of Bella, a red Toy Poodle, who is the main character of this book.

Although not blessed with their own children, Jennifer and Chris have several nieces, nephews, and Godchildren whom they love to spoil and spend their time.

Jennifer has a Bachelor's Degree in Psychology and a Master's Degree in Clinical Social Work. She currently works in corporate training and leadership development.

Turn that Frown Upside Down and *The Magical Unicorn* are two simultaneously published books by Jennifer. Both books are the first of two separate children's book series: *Bella's Adventures* and *The Three Little Girls*.

To send comments or inquire about upcoming books, please send an email to gervasebensonbooks@yahoo.com.